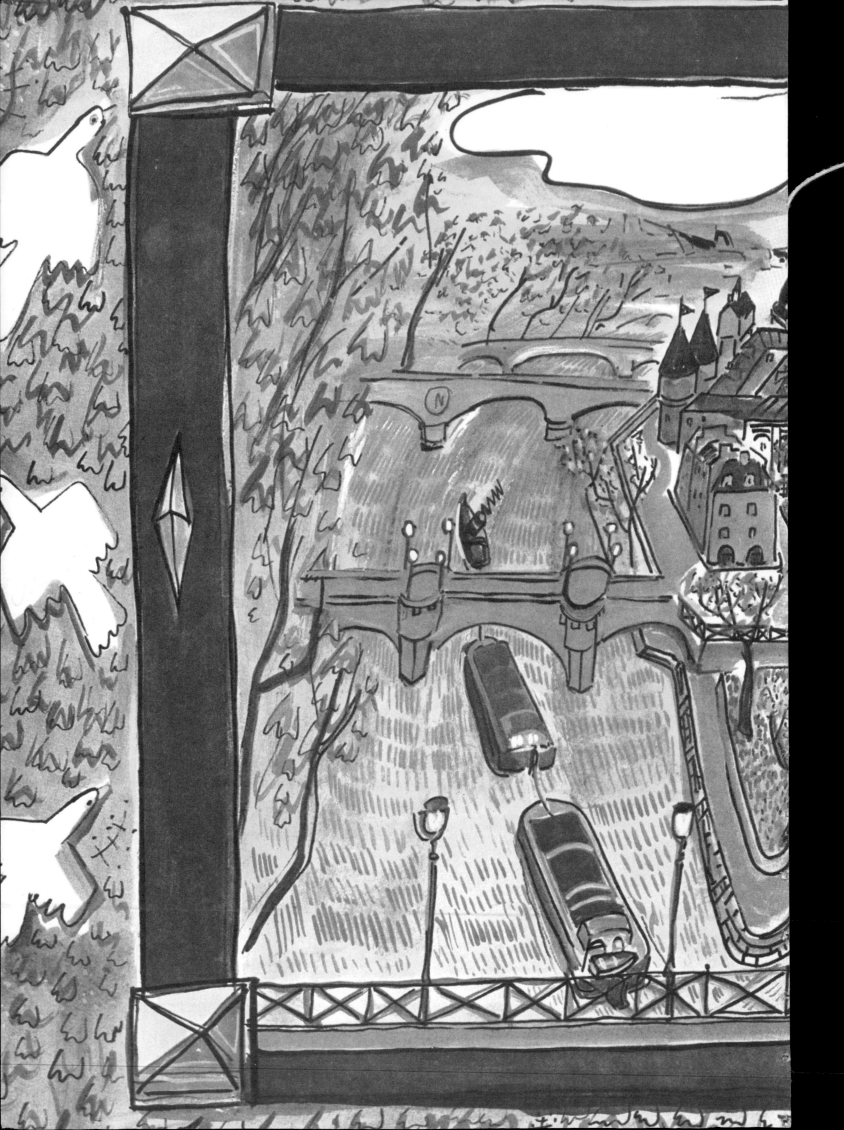

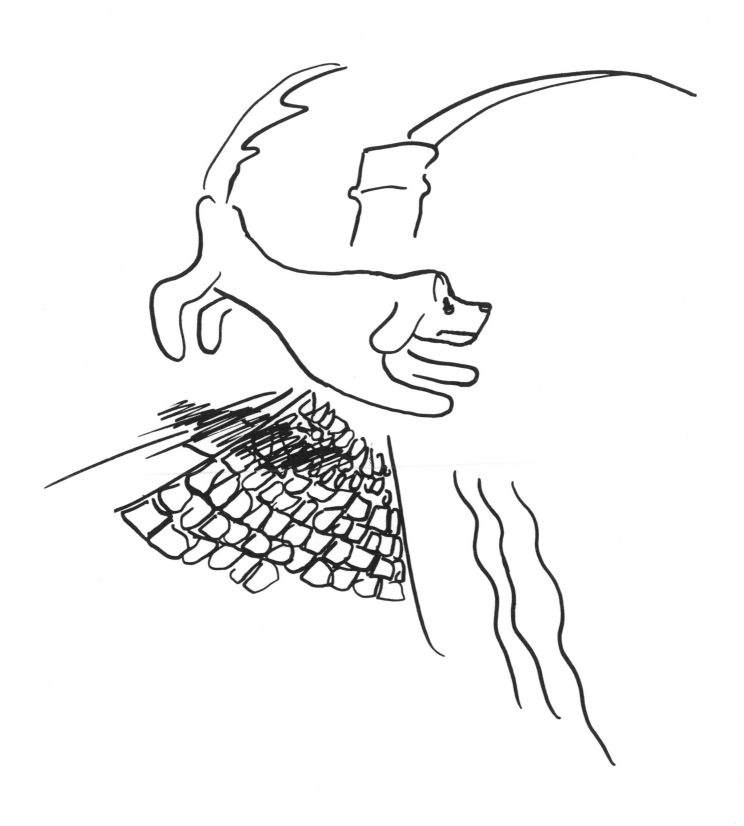

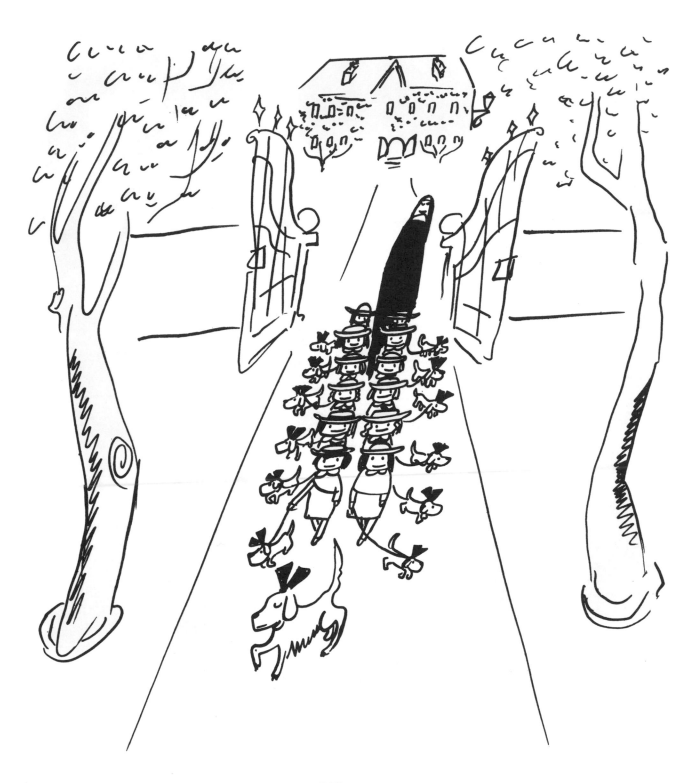

THE END

To go all around.

That suddenly there was enough hound

And to her surprise she found

For the third time that night
Miss Clavel turned on the light,

When Miss Clavel had stopped the riot
She thought, "At last we'll have some quiet."

"If there's one more fight about Genevieve,
I'm sorry, but she'll have to leave!"

And even faster.

And afraid of a disaster,
She ran fast—

For a second time that night
Miss Clavel turned on her light,

Miss Clavel turned out the light,
And again there was a fight,
While the children hugged her tight.
"Genevieve is *mine* tonight!"

"Good night, little girls, I hope you sleep well."
"Good night, good night, dear Miss Clavel!"

She was petted, she was fed,
And everybody went to bed.

Under an old street lamp outside
Genevieve sat alone and cried.

In the middle of the night
Miss Clavel turned on the light.
She said, "Something is not right."

"Oh, Genevieve, where can you be?
Genevieve, please come back to me."

Hours after they had started
Home they plodded broken-hearted.

The gendarmes said, "We don't believe
We've seen a dog like Genevieve."

But no dog came.

They called and called,

In every place they called her name

In every place a dog might go.

and low

They went looking high

"It's no use crying and no use talking
Let's get dressed and go out walking.
The sooner we're ready, the sooner we'll leave—
The sooner we'll find Miss Genevieve."

Madeline jumped on a chair.
"Lord Cucuface," she cried, "beware!
Miss Genevieve, noblest dog in France,
You shall have your VEN-GE-ANCE!"

"Away with you, you beastly hound!
And don't come back and hang around."

"I daresay," said Lord Cucuface.
"But it's really a disgrace
For young ladies to embrace
A creature of uncertain race!"

"Miss Clavel, get rid of it, please,"
Said the head of the board of trustees.
"Yes, but the children love her so,"
Said Miss Clavel. "Don't make her go."

Tap, tap! "Whatever can that be?"
Tap, tap! "Come out and let me see!"
"Dear me! A dog! But there's a rule
That says: NO DOGS ALLOWED IN SCHOOL."

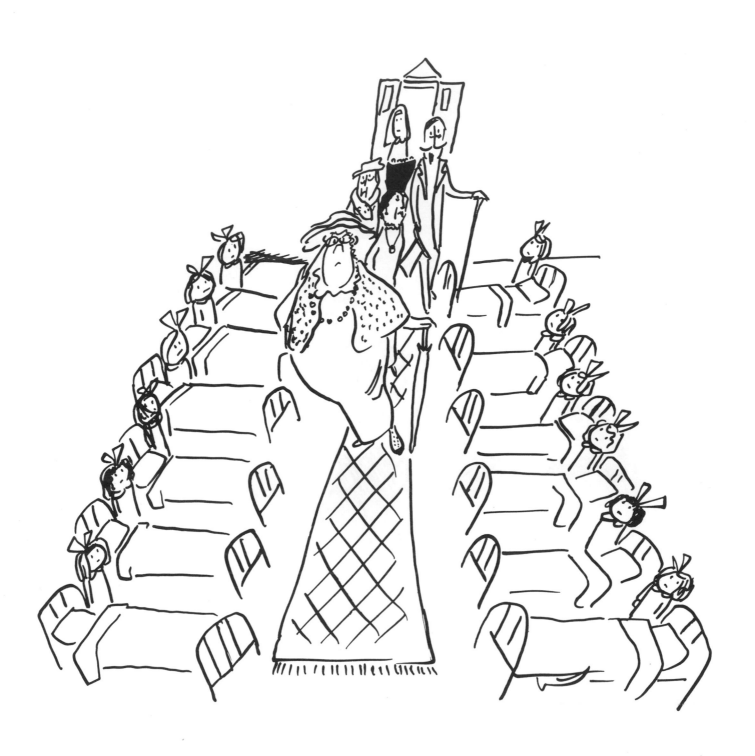

It was the annual inspection,
They were a very odd collection.

For on that day come wind or weather
The trustees all arrived together.

Every year the first of May
Was a very frightening day.

Soon the snow began to fly,
But the house was warm and dry
And six months passed quickly by.

And enjoyed the daily walk.

She could sing and almost talk

They never wanted her to leave
And they called her Genevieve.
The dog loved biscuits, bones and meat.
They sat around and watched her eat.

The new pupil was ever
So helpful and clever.

Miss Clavel turned out the light.
After she left there was a fight
About where the dog should sleep that night.

"Good night, little girls—I hope you sleep well."
"Good night, good night, dear Miss Clavel!"

"And here is a cup of camomile tea."

"In future I hope you will listen to me,"

So home they took the dog so brave.

And dragged her safe from a watery grave.

That kept its head

But for a dog

Poor Madeline would now be dead

Until the day she slipped and fell.

And nobody knew so well
How to frighten Miss Clavel—

In an old house in Paris that was covered in vines
Lived twelve little girls in two straight lines.
They left the house at half-past nine
In two straight lines in rain or shine.
The smallest one was MADELINE.
She was not afraid of mice.
She loved winter, snow and ice.
To the tiger in the zoo
Madeline just said, "Pooh pooh!"

Scholastic Children's Books,
Commonwealth House, 1-19 New Oxford Street,
London WC1A 1NU, UK
a division of Scholastic Ltd

London ~ New York ~ Toronto ~ Sydney ~ Auckland
Mexico City ~ New Delhi ·· Hong Kong

This story first appeared in Good Housekeeping
First published in the US by The Viking Press, Inc, 1953
First published in the UK by André Deutsch Ltd, 1953
This edition published by Scholastic Ltd, 1997

ISBN 0 590 19364 3

Printed in China

MADELINE'S
RESCUE

Story and pictures by

Ludwig Bemelmans

Also by Ludwig Bemelmans

MADELINE'S RESCUE